— FINDING —
GEMS

AN ILLUSTRATED STORY
BY DAN KUBISHTA

Preface

This book has been a labor of six years. The idea originated as a screenplay for a movie, and the novelization happened somewhat organically. I had always wanted to write a full-length book, yet the subject matter eluded me. Finally, I decided that the best course of action was just to write, and so I did. I wrote and wrote, by hand, the entire manuscript that you are now holding in your hands. This story has gone through numerous edits to get to the stage where it is today. Now I can honestly say that I have put down a solid story. It is based loosely on my own experience, but largely it is fiction. I hope that your experience reading *Finding Gems* is one that gives you value. I have found insight in reading for as long as I can remember, and it is my great pleasure to introduce to you this book.

Dan Kubishta
July 2021
Pacific Northwest

THE SETTING

An island located on the Pacific Ocean is where this story is mostly set. It has many different residents, a large city, and vast nature reserves. The place is called Brisby and Canby, among other names, and often it is referred to as simply The Island. The people work hard there, making the place almost entirely self-sufficient. Cargo ships and cruise liners are seen regularly, and many events are held there. The climate is semi-tropical.

Introduction

Max felt a hot breath above him. Incapacitated with a crippled limb, he looked up and into the eyes of a fully grown and very bothered tiger. Gemstones shone nearby.

"First to the prize," came a voice.

"Ned," said Max. "It's not worth it."

A tiger cub ran by. Its mother roared.

CHAPTER ONE
FIVE DAYS EARLIER

A MONDAY IN JUNE
MODERN-DAY

Evening rays of golden sunbeams skipped across the sea's weathered surface. Atop it, there traveled a single passenger ship named Anne. The light that was over the area's Pacific waters had come after a brief tumultuous swell. The massive and swift currents of the vast ocean's pounding heart had subsided now, and the sea was very calm. The ship bobbed.

The vessel had been painted exclusively white. It shone like a magic glistening star. The ship was not ancient, but the contrary. She was state of the art, and no masts laden with billowing sails were to be seen from the deck.

Soon, Anne would sit securely in the harbor's restraints. Now though, Anne had still been worked to deliver the final leg of that journey. Aboard, dinner had just ended. There had been a brim of excitement as the island of Brisby no longer seemed a distant prospect.

Now there had gathered a good number of passengers on the top deck, bustling with a combination of impatience and excitement. They were ranging in diversity, with the more elite being granted access seats for the night's top deck fest.

There was a young man, Max by name, who didn't even come *close* to landing one of those magenta seats.

Now he wandered like a loitering lizard, beneath the party. Checking his steps, carefully striding, he glanced over to the red curtain that divided him from the stairwell leading up to the top deck. The curtain remained steadily closed. *Trifles*, he thought. Of course, Max wasn't the only one down there. Anne carried a large number of travelers, and that piece of venue on the top? Well, limited. Limited.

Soon, singing began. The voices were distinct, like trumpets.

"A brass blaze of benny notes bluffing," one bystander observed.

The vocalists revealed the song's studded wordplay:

BRISTOL'S BROWN EYES HAD BEEN FULL
OF SURPRISE
ON THAT MORNING IN TRUE BLUE
SEPTEMBER
THEN, SHE HAD BEEN TROUBLED AS HER
MIND WANDERED COUPLED
WITH THOUGHTS LAYING DISTANT HER
MEMORY

Max walked over to the guardrails installed at the ship's edges, listening to the music as the sun set shrinking behind him, gold. He stood very still, watching the ocean as it swelled.

2

NED

Above Max stood a figure shrouded in blackness. Then, the figure stepped into the light. It was a porter by the name of Ned. Security was what he was in charge of mostly, but he often left his post to seek fun. Currently, he seemed to be doing his job quite well though, walking with purpose across the breadth of the platforms. He looked down. He saw Max then and made a face. Max and

Ned had once gone to school together, but they had never been friends. Not even close.

3

BACKSTORY OF MAX

Max now saw the island off in the distance. It crystallized in his vision, and he thought to himself: *Finally here! Let's do this!*

Max was going to Brisby to work. He flipped back the cuff of his white shirt to reveal a silver watch. It had been a gift from his mother some time ago. As he read the time, his memory drifted back to where this journey had initially begun.

Max and his sister Penny had lived, with their mother, in a quaint little house back on the mainland. The status of the household had been mostly peaceful, but in recent times the question of dollars became prominent for them, what with the economy falling fickle.

There was no father figure present. Even though their mother had managed to keep her job amidst the faltering economic climate, she was not the wealthiest of women by any stretch of the imagination. Max was beginning to think his future would be abysmal if he stayed in that place, and so he actively searched out opportunities. Also, Penny was now ill with some strange ailment, and the doctor bills were piling up. He wanted to help her.

It was December then, and during that month a knock on the door was heard. Penny answered the door and upon opening it was surprised to see her Aunt Kat. Kat was their mother's sister  who had gone off to live in Brisby years ago. She did have the habit of dropping by, usually unannounced, for visits with the children and her mother. Kat was a kind person, and although her sister considered her lovable, she often felt like she took it too far. One such instance of this was the current situation, for she had brought along with her a fellow by the name of Timothy Green. Max's mother sighed, but let them in.

"Let me introduce myself, everyone!" Mr. Green said.

They were all standing in the parlor.

"I am Timothy
Green, gem smith,
and I have long
been friends with
your darling aunt."

He was wearing a vest that was way
too small for him and his hair was black,
slicked professionally with various
pomades. Max liked Mr. Green. The
middle-aged man talked about a great
deal of things during his short stay there,
and one of these things was an
employment possibility for Max.

"You know," Mr. Green had said.
"A lot of people on the island just don't
want to work for whatever reason. There
is a lot of work to be done for sure,
mining mostly. I am the boss for much of

12

the island's quarries. The city is advancing and the mining operation, of which I am a head, is gearing up for the summer season."

"Mining?" questioned Max.

"Don't let that term scare you. 'Gem Technician' is what I like to call them. The money is real and plentiful in any case, if you're willing to put in the work, and a job could be yours if you're willing to travel there."

Max was intrigued but had his reservations. Go to Brisby?

"It would be well worth the summer, in my humble opinion," said Mr. Green, adjusting his glasses.

"I don't know," Max said without thinking.

"If you're not sold on it, I could offer you a discounted ticket to the place. Due to military restrictions, there isn't air travel at this time, but there are cruise lines still running."

"Aye," Max agreed.

"It's not too long of a trip, two days at the most. Trust me, the cruise is fun!"

Max was sold. Mr. Green was catching his breath. Kat sat him down in a chair.

"He gets excited about things," she informed.

Kat's mother looked over – she had been listening to the conversation as well. Penny was playing with a dog in the yard.

Kat said, "He could stay at my place for the duration of the summer. What do you think, Suzanne?"

Max looked to his mother. Suzanne said, "It's your decision, Max. Don't let me stop you. You're twenty-one years old, old enough to do adult things."

Max smiled. He had never been on a cruise ship before.

The watch was ticking. Max covered the piece once again with his shirt's cuff. He looked up. Brisby was very close. In a flashing instant he saw a sharp glimmer of city lights, but his attention was soon snapped back to the ship's activity. The singing had stopped, and there was now a strange, low energy afoot. Voices talked above Max.

4

MR. PRICE AND THE CAPTAIN

Ned was conversing with his boss, Mr. Aldous M. Price. Mr. Price was the owner of the ship, and indeed of an entire fleet of cruise liners. There was standing by the two another. It was Lawrence, the ship's captain.

"Where is that cap that I gifted you?" asked Mr. Price.

Ned sighed, looking upward. His copper tufts of hair flapped in the breeze, free of any restriction that a cap might cause.

"Cap?"

"Who is this person?" asked the captain, very annoyed.

"Ned's the name, sir!"

"He's the newly hired porter," Mr. Price added.

"Ah! A porter. I can recall when I was in your position. Not a bad time but still, I don't miss it!"

Lawrence was a kindly gentleman with a thin grey mustache that added to his air of importance. His eyes twinkled as he spoke, and his whole demeanor conveyed experience and wisdom.

"Of all the captains I have traveled with, you are the best one," Mr. Price praised. "Thank you for another fine voyage."

"An honor, to be sure! Now, let's go to the passengers who wait."

Aldous and Lawrence started down a stairwell, leaving Ned behind. Mr.

Price looked back and said, "Hurry, Ned! The passengers need to be told how to exit, and they may need luggage assistance!"

5

THE SISTERS

From somewhere on the deck, a flash of piercing brightness came forth and blinded Max. A shiny garment worn by a young woman named Colette Price was the culprit. Colette was a daughter of Aldous. The garment she wore was beautiful. It had sockets for arms and a

18

fastening band that lay secure across Colette's chest. As she walked, the garment shimmered, swinging with opulent weight. She strode up to a girl standing at a guardrail and began to converse with her. Max, who was still watching, recognized both of them. Colette had been a singer that evening, and the girl who talked to her now was her sister. Max had never sat at the table these girls sat at in the dining hall. *Trifles*, he thought again. The girls didn't see Max because he was standing opposite them and a good distance away as well. Max left to gather his luggage, weaving through the crowded spaces.

"It sounded fine from where I was sitting," said the girl beside Colette. Her hair was tied up into a bun with a pink ribbon and her eyes were full of optimism. Her name was Evelyn-Paige Price, but most of the time she went by simply Paige.

"Thank you," said Colette.

Paige was in her own world, where she spent most of her time. She almost smiled when she saw her sister's performance get-up. On most, it would have seemed distastefully gaudy.

I wouldn't stand in line to put that thing on, Paige mused. Paige was not much like her sister, not wanting to go on stage yet bored to the core with monotonous tasks. Her character was strong and sweet while retaining the strength of a diamond. Her lips were pale red and her face stern as she watched the sun offering the last light of the day. Shallow rushes of sea-air wind swept over the guardrails, and strands of Paige's blonde hair were caught up in the movement.

Colette was still talking, and Paige was still thinking.

I wonder whether our bosun will ever let me job shadow. Anne's relatively more important workings, that would be interesting. This journey has been taxing.

The sisters walked across the deck to view the island's harbor. Max stood nearby, resting an arm on a suitcase. Paige heard her name being called. She turned and saw Max. She turned away from Max, and the next thing she saw was her father Aldous coming down the steps hastily.

6

GUARDIAN

The sun disappeared completely into the west then, revealing Brisby's shimmering skyline. Mr. Price was talking to Paige.

"Back to Brisby," he was saying. "These trips never get old. For you they might."

"It's ok," Paige said. "This will probably be the last time for a while."

"You're much like your mother in not liking to move around so much."

Mr. Price stood pensive and watchful.

"Be safe as always, Paige."

"Father, I'm twenty-two, almost twenty-three. I know how to conduct myself; you know."

"I know," said Aldous. "Still, I will always remember you as that little girl who looked to me for protection when she was young. While I'm still around, you can bet that I'll act now as I did then. Nobody, nobody hurts Paige on my watch."

Paige gave her father a hug.

"I heard you have quite the birthday soiree planned when you get back?"

"Quite," answered Paige, glowing.

7

LIBBY

Ned stood at the guard rail. He was speaking now with a young woman with black hair, green eyes, and overall bright good looks. Her name was Libby, and she was on a small vacation to get away from corporate life.

"Here already Libby," said Ned.

Libby nodded. "Glad to hear it."

"So you're visiting some family on the island?"

"Yes, well. I've never met them before in person, so it should be interesting. Also, you know how I needed a bit of time away from the office."

"Perhaps we'll see each other again after you're done visiting. I'm never on the island for too long. While I am though, I'll offer my tour guide skills, if you'll take them."

Ned was an unofficial tour guide of the island for many of the fleet's travelers. He liked being able to show people around and show off how good he thought he was at doing it. Recently, he had set his sights on providing the service to Colette and Paige, and Paige very specifically. It was not because he loved her. He was trying to marry Paige for obvious reasons, not the least being a portion of an inheritance that included a fleet of cruise ships! That was his plan, anyway. No one ever said it was a foolproof one.

"I still help the Price sisters find their way around the city, and they've been here multiple times. I know all the best spots, I can assure you."

"Thanks! I will consider it!"

Libby turned because she felt an energy. Max was thirty feet away. Ned looked too.

"That guy," said Libby. "He nearly took my jewelry yesterday when it was sitting on my table in the dining hall. Luckily I swatted his hand before he made off with it."

"He just tried to blatantly steal it?"

"To be fair, I don't think he entirely realized it was mine since I wasn't seated. It was only when I caught him out of the corner of my eye that I realized he was trying to take it for keeps."

"Max is his name," said Ned, "and I don't like 'em."

8

WELCOME TO BRISBY

Captain Lawrence let the passengers know: it was safe to exit! They did then, in single file lines. Cameras flashed. The island seemed to welcome the visitors, but an ominous pall was present. One traveler thought he saw a mermaid in the water. In the now near distance, the lights of Brisby's cosmopolitan city shone bright. On the shore, tall black trees of varying shapes stood silhouetted against the night sky, waving.

Max walked forward with momentum. One of his steps was dramatic. It was the step that bridged the gap between the ramp leading the passengers off the ship and the stony path that lay flatly installed on the island's beach.

Soon, all the passengers had disembarked. The moon was out, full, and it illuminated the name of the ship that was printed out neatly on its side: A.N.N.E. Anne was to set in the harbor for around seventy-two hours – that was enough time to let the crew unwind before doing it all again!

Now, everyone worked to find various modes of transport to take them to all corners of the island. Some took buses, some took cabs, some took private limousines. All though, had one thing in common: they were excited.

Max hailed a cab to transport him. He got in and looked ahead.

"Where to?" asked a kindly driver. Max told him.

Soon, they rolled up to a checkpoint. It was actually part of a larger complex that was placed right in front of

the city's metropolitan border. The cab
driver lowered the window and looked
over. Personnel sat behind the counters,
wearing very official badges. A raven flew
overhead, looking for shiny objects.

"Authorization. Identification.
Permits...permits! Please."
Max provided the documents
then, grabbing them out of his suitcase.
The process was being carried out near
all the checkpoint windows. Cars rolled
up, and the question was like a demand.
"Papers!"
Max had given the official a few
pieces of identification, including a
passport. The official looked at Max, and
then at the photo ID. He shook his head,
stamped a mermaid insignia on one of
the pages, and handed it back.
"You're good. Enjoy Brisby!"

The driver gave a thumbs up and looked at the official, then over to Max.

"Welcome," he stated warmly before slamming on the gas pedal.

"Welcome," he said again.

There was, however, more protocol.

"Stop!" came a voice. The vehicle was searched.

"Orders," said an official with large eyes. The driver muttered a phrase beneath earshot.

"You're good," came a voice after a few minutes.

The car drove through a tall entrance.

"Welcome," said the driver. "My favorite place in all the world."

In less than thirty minutes they were there. Kat's place had recently been converted into an inn, with quarters for about ten guests, give or take. *Dazing Inn* was what it was called.

9

THE INN

Neon letters spelled out the words "Dazing Inn" positioned above the building's entrance. The sign fit in well with the rest of the property's laissez-faire vibe. On the front lawns, guests sat mingling. Mostly, they sat at sleek tables.

The tables had been stacked albeit not highly stacked with cool mulberry shandies and mixed bowls of eateries such as strawberries, crackers, and cheese. Everything was dimly lit by the lights of standing torches. Fireflies hummed low to the ground.

The cab had driven off, and now Max was standing on the sidewalk in front of the yard alone with his luggage. There could be heard the nearby sound of a guitar rifting soft blues. Electric. Max walked slowly on the path that led to the place's doors.

"Max?" The voice was Kat's.

He looked to his left and saw his aunt getting up from a table where she had been socializing.

"There he is! My Max!" She crossed over the lawn to complete the greeting.

"A choice summer evening, no?"

"Indeed," Max affirmed.

"Something fresh to drink? Come, I'll show you your accommodations. Follow me."

Max did, and Kat began to inform him of what to expect. They made their way up the small flight of stairs, onto the inn's porch, and inside the sweeping establishment. Off to the side in a little nook sat an attractive blonde working on a tablet. Her name was Liliane Camden, and she managed the inn's affairs when Kat was off doing other things.

"I was talking to Mr. Green a few days ago," Kat said. "I hope you've come ready for work! Mr. Green as you probably could tell was not very stringent, but he does require some certifications to be presented to him."

"Certifications?"

"You can get them at the bureau of the city. It's just so that you'll be able to work officially on Brisby!"

"When do I get them?"

"Tomorrow! I can drive you to the bureau on my way into the city."

10
The Bureau
Tuesday

As the light of morning's beckoning was dispersing the fireflies' luminescence, Max and Kat left the inn.

"Today's a big day, no?"

Max responded to Kat with a friendly yawn, and they were off.

The city streets were crowded. Kat wove in and out of traffic skillfully and soon they arrived at the bureau. Max got out with his paperwork and noticed that there was a slight balm in the air.

"I will have to leave you," said Kat. "Can you find your way to Rose's Flowers after you get certifications?"

"Yes," said Max. "You'll be there?"

"I'll be there."

The car drove away. Max stood at the front of the bureau building.

11

LOST BRIEFCASE

At the island's ritziest hotel, *The Empress,* Lawrence sat at a table in the dining room sipping on a cup of hot goodness. Out of his periphery he saw Aldous rushing past him.

"Oh no!" Aldous was saying to himself.

"Where are you off to?" Lawrence cried.

"To find my briefcase!" Aldous stopped suddenly and then said even more seriously, "My concierge must have overlooked it. "

"The porter?"

"Aye," said Aldous, and he turned to run towards the parking lot.

He met with a driver named Jay.

"The transit center, Jay," Aldous spoke.

The car left. Mr. Price looked out at the familiar sights that passed by him. He had within the last few years considered Brisby less of a stop and more of a home away from his permanent residence.

12

AT THE TRANSIT CENTER

"We don't have it," said the person at the counter.

Aldous groaned. *That new porter*, he thought. *He had one job…*

"We'll keep an eye out for it though."

"More than an eye," Aldous replied. "Can you send out a search for it? I'm fairly sure my concierge left it on the bus that drove my crew and I to the Hotel Empress last night. That briefcase is important to me, very important!"

"Of course," said the worker. Pressing a button, she spoke evenly.

"Briefcase lost by Aldous Price of Price Fleets. Color?"

"Blue, navy blue," said Aldous.

"Dimensions?"

"20 by 9 inches," he answered.

"Bus?"

"I think it was bus 4, I could be wrong."

A few moments passed slowly.

"Yes," came a voice from the other end. "It's here."

"Can you bring it back to the transit center?"

"No," said the voice. "It will have to wait. I've got a busload of tourists who will not be happy if I turn around. It will be returned when we get back to the east side of the island, in about four days' time."

Libby sat on that bus along with the tourists. She peered out of a glazed window. The lush surroundings zipped by.

"Four days?" cried Aldous. "I have to leave sooner than that unless I delay the entire return trip!" He was almost blue in the face.

The worker blinked. The voice on the other end muffled and faded.

"Four days," said the worker.

13

THE GUIDE

Brisby's city had been constructed in a very smart way. Centrally located was a beautiful park. At the park, there were areas for leisure as well as marketplaces for selling. There were a variety of stands and shops, touting everything from plump oranges to clothes to technology to produce. There was a good deal of items that especially caught the view of many a passerby, mostly the giant bright lemons, ornate pocket watches, big decorative books, and flower arrangements of a hundred different colors. The area's grounds had been covered completely in a roll of natural and green grass carpet, and it ran in a groove border up along the edges of the pebbly paths and the lines of hued hedgerows.

Some people sat conversing on blankets atop the lawns while others perused the market. Music streamed across the entire park. On this Tuesday morning, the weather was balmy as well as sunny, but not in the least bit miserable.

Just then, a blue cab had pulled up to a curb on the park's outer side. Three persons left the cab behind and walked together up the paved lanes of the park. These three were Paige, Colette, and Ned.

"Here it is again," said Ned. "The great park!"

The girls asked him some questions about the place. The three walked down the main path, stopping every so often to look at various stalls that they were interested in. One of the places they had stopped to linger at for a moment was Brisby's premier flower shop.

"Welcome to Rose's Flowers!" said Kat. She was there for a while to help her friend out.

"These are lovely arrangements," said Colette.

"I agree. We're trying to get some more arranged for the gala on Thursday night."

"Gala?"

"Oh yes, it's a very important event for us Brisbanes. You must be tourists."

"Yeah," said Colette and Paige together.

"The gala's epic," Ned said.

"Music, sports, dancing, shows, fireworks! Oh, the fireworks!"

"When and where will this gala be?"

"At the pavilion," said Kat, indicating a section of the park nearby.

"Thursday night at 6 'o clock."

"Oh, we won't be here," said Paige. "Trifles."

"Thank you anyhow," said Colette, grabbing a bunch of orchids and bringing them to the counter. "I want these."

43

Paige brought some up too, and by the time they were done buying them, Ned had disappeared.

"Where did he go," Colette said.

He materialized (or so it seemed) a few moments later.

"What happened?" asked Paige.

"Nothing," Ned insisted.

14

TIN, LIEUTENANT AND OFFICER

Aldous stepped out of a parked cab onto the stone curb in front of the city's law enforcement building.

"Thank you, Jay," he said.

Soon, he was meeting with Officer Lieutenant Tin.

"I'll shake your hand, old friend!"

"Good to see you again," said Aldous.

"My polished buttons. You as well, Aldy! How was your journey here?

"The usual," he replied. "The usual except my briefcase with all my important documents were left on a bus that isn't coming back to this side of the island for four days! Four days, can you believe it! I talked to the transit center and that's the best they could do."

"Well, the transit center is usually quite adequate as far as the recovering of objects is concerned aboard their own buses, Aldous."

"Yes. Still though, can you keep a lookout?"

"Of course, old friend!"

15

ROSE

Max was making his way down a cobbled path, looking for Rose's Flowers. He held the papers that had been handed to him at the bureau after some deliberation on their part. Very soon though, he found the shop and saw a familiar face.

"Max!" said Kat. "The directions I gave you worked, however meager they might've been...I knew you'd find it."

"I have the papers."

"Great," Kat replied. "Before you go running off to see Mr. Green, I have a favor to ask you."

"Okay," said Max, glancing down at his watch.

"I need to stay here to finish up some things, but my friend Rose would really appreciate it if you could help deliver some floral arrangements to a hotel."

"Is that her real name?"

Kat gave Max a funny look.

"She's in the back, preparing the deliveries. Follow me."

The plan seemed sensible enough to Max. Max was shown to the area behind the shop. At first, all he saw were tall trees that formed a wall. Max walked up to a gate that was built into the wall and peered in, for the gate was not solid stone but wrought iron, and he could see through the spaces between each rod a garden inside of the little fortress what contained it. He opened the gate's door, walked forward, and the door behind him swung gentle and shutting without his aid. As the door made a murmuring clamp, he looked over his right shoulder. Kat was on the outside, waving. Max gulped, but he soon was relieved. His eyes now drank in the sights around him. Everywhere there were masses of flowering blossom bunches. There were hundreds of stargazer lilies with their adornments of red and blue, and orchids blooming brilliantly. There were clock flowers and hibiscus varieties, red and yellow roses, and a type of tulip variation that almost looked like they were clad in sleeves of ruffled extravagance. Max was in awe. Hovering here and there above the arrays were a good number of buzzing bee things. The movement of these pollinating machine's wings was very much like a helicopter's functioning.

There was a noise then, like someone stepping on some crunchy leaves. The little helicopters scattered in midair as someone walked into the garden. It was Ms. Rose herself in the flesh.

The young woman was twenty-five. Her hair was a light mahogany, cut in an elegantly styled manner to frame her face's features. She had eyes that elongated with eloquent temper. The lids, laden with heavily dropping lashes, were moving off to one side as the woman strode into the place, commanding Max's attention. She'd applied some time earlier a bit of lipstick, and her face seemed to resemble a flower if it was possible.

"Follow me, Max," Ms. Rose chanted. She took some flowers to her car, a pretty little vehicle, parked very close to the garden. Her arms were carefully folding across the bouquets, lending support like a rose's stem does.

16

THE NATURAL PARK

The floral arrangements that were to be delivered were soon all loaded into the car. Max and Rose had made good time, and now they both got into the car.

"You've got a sweet ride," said Max.

"I've just bought it," responded Rose. "I've always wanted this little car."

She pressed down on the gas pedal and they drove off towards the hotel. *The Empress*.

On the way, they drove past a natural park. It housed many animals that would probably not survive in the wild, except for the tigers. They were ferocious. The natural park was an oasis on the outskirts of the city. It had massive botanical gardens, butterfly sanctuaries, and an aviary.

The car zoomed by.

17

MAX AND NED

The car stopped. Ms. Rose then explained what was happening at the hotel.

"Some dignitaries will be discussing matters of great importance. Great importance to them. There's a welcome meeting with a banquet in the dining hall. We provide the flowers, they provide the class. Tongue-in-cheek, Max...you'll get the hang of it."

Max smiled. He might have been in love with Ms. Rose already.

Her heels clicked as she walked through the door, laden with flowers galore. Max held flowers now too, and he looked up at the grand hotel before he went into the place. It was truly an impressive hotel.

They entered the dining hall, and Max helped her decorate the tables.

"I appreciate it, Max. You're a gem."

When they were getting closer to finishing the project, guests started to stream in from the lobby. Rose was managing a trying array when she recognized one of the guests. He had talked with her that morning...

Ned had greeted Rose politely.

"Hi, you are decorating the dignitary banquet tomorrow, right?"

"Yes," Rose had said.

"Right. I have a special request. There's a room that someone is staying in whom I would like to surprise. Room 216, I want it decked out with flowers and garlands, all around the door frame."

"Yes, we can do that for an extra charge."

"Great! We'll be down in the dining hall around 12:30, so it would be best to do it then. Would you also mind attaching this card?"

"We can do that."

Rose motioned to Max.

"Max, honey."

"Yes?"

"Could you take the garland in the trunk of the car and the card laying next to it up to room 216 and decorate it? It's a special favor."

"Okay!"

It was 12:25.

Max ran out to the car, found the decoration along with the card (inside of a beige envelope), and was moments later decorating the door. The garland was woven with dozens of red roses, and it really was a good decoration. Max didn't notice at first, however, that the door to room 216 was actually open a bit. Paige was inside, and she moved towards the door, wondering what the commotion was about.

"What's this?" she asked.

Max looked at her.

"Flower delivery," Max said.

"For me? Hey, I've seen you before. Did you come here on the cruise liner Anne?"

Paige took out a rose to swirl from the garland and waited for Max's reply.

"I did."

Suddenly, Ned came hurrying down the hallway towards the room. Ned. If this book was a movie, the director would have imposed a quick edit zoom to focus on Ned's facial features. They were at first normal, albeit a bit frustrated, but then turned from surprise, to anger, and gradually into rage. He halted midstep. He saw now his delivery request being botched in real time. Then he recognized Max.

"Paige," he started. "What time is it?"

"What?"

"What time is it?" It was more like a demand this time.

"I know I'm late. I just had to get a few of my things ordered and polished shining."

"Yes, you're late."

Paige could read Ned.

"What's the matter?"

Max stood holding the garland.

"Did you ask for these to be delivered to me, Ned?"

"Yes, but the reveal has been regrettably botched. It's all wrong!"

Ned had of course planned to show Paige to her room after the banquet. He fought to keep his head from flying off its proverbial handle. Max may have been dead meat if not for Paige's watchful gaze. Ned would not be uncivil around her. Ned turned to Max.

"I've seen you before, turnip."

Max scrunched his eyebrows as Ned continued to a monologue.

"The delivery person was not to be knock-knock 'a knocking on this door, friend. If I were a sheriff in this town, you'd be in trouble. This delivery was doomed when they asked you to do it, sir. Next time, you let your lady boss do the job, and she'll do it right."

Paige went back into the room to quickly grab her things.

"I'm just here to deliver these flowers, don't want any problems."

Paige's eyes were passing from Ned to Max.

"My condolences," said Max.

Ned took a step forward that was long enough to where he now stood face to face with Max. Their faces were not more than three inches apart.

"These roses here were to be hung on the doorframe here, as per my requesting, and to ensure that they get hung, I myself will personally do the task. Is that clear, turnip?"

Paige walked to the doorframe again and Ned moved away.

"I'm ready, Ned."

Ned took the garland from Max gently. "As you were."

Max walked away.

Ned sulked as he slowly hung up the rest of the garland. Paige opened up the envelope.

WELCOME MS. PRICE
TO THE ISLAND OF BRISBY
THE GREAT ISLE OF SPECTACULARITIES
ROSES ARE RED, MY FRIEND, VIOLETS
THEY SAY ARE BLUE, AND WHITE?
THE COLOR OF LILIES
MAKE SURE TO NOTE, ON THIS NOTE,
THAT I'VE WROTE
THAT MY HELP HAS NO BOUNDS 'CEPT
LIABILITIES

"Shall we?" said Ned. He offered Paige his elbow and she put her white-gloved hand on it as they made their way to the elevator.

Max was on the ground floor once again, and he met up with Ms. Rose, who was gathering the last scraps of unused bouquet material. They got into her car, and they drove away from the hotel. As Max looked out of the passenger side window, he saw for the last time that day the gates to the natural park. Sitting on top of the steel bars was a stone statuette of a snarling tiger. It seemed gargoyle-like, and although frozen in time, it seemed to wave its paws in ferocious warning movements. Max looked away.

18

GREEN'S GEMS

Mr. Green had been talking with a customer when Max and Kat had entered his store through the front. They walked over to Timothy's counter, but he did not notice them until after some shoppers had left.

"Hello, Kat!"

Kat looked at Timothy, then at Max.

"Oh, hello! Jams of a jillion options, I didn't even see you, my boy! Max, isn't it?"

Handshakes. Twice.

"Welcome to Brisby, savvy lad. This is it! Homebase for the gem business here. Green's Gems."

Max looked around.

"A thing of beauty, isn't it? However, this isn't where you'll be working. The quarries are outside of the city. The person who is the expert of all that is a man by the name of Marco. You'll be reporting to him when you're on the worksite. I'll be here most days if you need anything. I wave a finger on this island and things get done. So much to do, so little time; always the problem my boy."

It was around closing time, and most of the customers had left the shop. There was a faint buzz of energy in the room, and Max could hear his heart beating softly in his chest.

"Marco's not here now," Mr. Green continued, "but in the morning when you come in, 8 'o clock if you would, make sure you leave with Marco. Then, it's off to the races for you...er, you did get employment certifications, right?"

Max nodded.

"Perfect. Other than that, I haven't much to say. Welcome aboard." He smiled.

Mr. Green had been standing while he talked, but now he went over to his chair, sat down, and pulled it up to the counter's edge. He was in the process of repairing some pieces for customers, mostly necklaces and rings.

"Kat! What do you make of this diamond here?"

He held up a gem that was rustically tarnished but was now in the process of being stripped, cleaned, and polished to shine.

"It's cool," said Kat. "You always do a good job."

"Kat, have a laugh. I'm no businessman lacking coherence in training, but neither am I a zebra of unlettered striping. How've you been?"

"You know me, just the usual! Say, I have a piece that would profit from the skilled hand of a smith, Tim."

"What?"

"A necklace. Had it for years but I'm afraid it's falling apart. A family heirloom actually, so I would not like to see it go uncared for."

"Bring it on down, and I'll work my magic on it."

19

THE NECKLACE

Later at Kat's place, the eccentric woman rounded the corner and walked into Max's room. He looked over and saw that she was bringing the necklace over to him.

"You've heard the stories of your great-grandfather James, right?"

Max nodded. "Some," he said.

"He was a soldier back during the first world war. What about the story about this necklace?"

Max shook his head.

"He kept this necklace with him throughout the entirety of his service."

Kat's eyes glazed as she remembered the stories she had been told. Her father had recalled them, and now images from his words rose again in vivid memory.

"By all accounts, James was a valiant man. He was there on the front lines."

20
THE WESTERN FRONT
FRANCE, 1917

Howling flares of black filled the pitch night sky. A flag wove strong above the battlefield. Orange and red were the primary colors that the soldiers saw as shells exploded everywhere. Two opposing forces were clashing. On a ridge, silhouettes of darkened figures rode silently amidst the screaming melee.

Farther down, a giant trench had been ripped forth from the coal-colored earth as the parched valley surrounding it had led it deep furrows across enemy lines. Many soldiers ran through the trench, rushing through its narrow passageway. Their feet seemed to weigh some of them down with each stride they attempted to make. From somewhere within the enemy's rigid ranks came forth a massive blasting force which laid claim to everything in its awful path. As the very sky rained hail of destruction, some of the soldiers climbed forth from out of the trench to seek safer positions.

"Get down, you fools!"

They didn't listen. As a mortar worked its destruction, James rescued six men from sure annihilation. Then, he was struck. Clutching the necklace that he had carried with him, a piece of jewelry that was his woman's, he found the strength to continue on for a little while longer. He saved two more men and was carried away by combat medics.

21

MISSING GEMS

"He held onto this necklace, they say, as he lay taking his final breaths in a hospital tent. It was his reminding object, he told his fellow soldiers, reminding him of why he fought. For freedom, he would say. For what was right. They sent this necklace back home to his wife when he passed, and so she regained what was once hers while at the same time losing that which was most dear. Somehow, it was passed on down to me, and I have kept it ever since, Max. Look though! It's in disrepair. It needs new gems."

Kat let a sigh come through her eyes. She lifted the necklace and looked at it. The chain that held the whole thing together could not be seen much, save for the exceedingly small distances beneath smooth beads. The most prominent feature was the oval-shaped locket fixture that seemed to give the necklace a certain elegant weight. It had tiny gems laid into the surface, but there were noticeable spots where it looked like the gems originally there had been somehow popped out.

"Here," said Kat. She gave Max the necklace. It sat on his outstretched palm. The next day, it was there again, and Mr. Green took the piece carefully. He lifted the necklace and saw its missing gems.

"I will fix it," said Mr. Green. "Marco and the crew are back behind the shop. You'll find them by the warehouse that houses all of the trucks."

Max headed out back then.

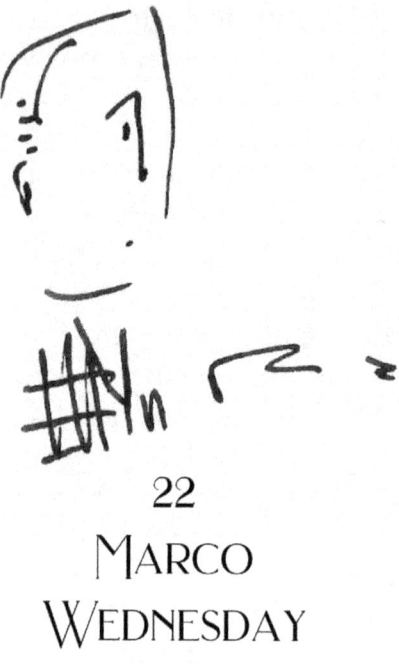

22

MARCO
WEDNESDAY

Max walked through the door out to the back lot where he was met with stares. Twenty-five or so miners and engineers looked over.

"Hello!" said Max.

Marco Mix, a solid-built man who certainly could throw a caber like no one's business, walked over to Max.

"This must be the newest recruit. You're from the mainland, aren't you?"

"That's right. Max is my name. You must be Marco?"

"My name's Marco," he affirmed whilst he flipped over the handle on his pickax hammer.

"Take a chair in my lair of a truck, you green tangerine of a recruit. Soon, you'll learn the ropes of necessity."

Max hopped. Marco revved the engine.

"Welcome to Brisby."

It took eight vehicles to transport everyone from the gem store to the quarry ten miles out from the city's east walls. When they got there, Marco got out of his truck and over to where a mule had been sitting, almost seeming to wait for him.

"Up on your cloved feet, Jules," said Marco.

The crew from Brisby's city was not the only crew; altogether there at the quarry were around fifty people. Marco sat now atop the mule, riding around giving instructions.

"Listen," he had told Max. "This quarry here is like the klondike. Tons of diamonds to be found. You though, are starting over there, where we harvest the fill."

"Fill?"

"It's the important material on a lot of jewelry that often goes unnoticed, but if there were no fill in some of the pieces, they'd just fall apart in an instant. Think of it as fool's gold, but not actually that."

"Yes, sir," said Max.

"Put in a hard day's work today. Tomorrow everyone's getting off early. The gala's on, and I'm going."

Max wasn't sure what to make of Marco. He looked up to the sky. Big black birds, buzzards, flew high above the site. They were seeking out snacks most definitely. The mining operation was going now with great gusto.

Rock and roll, Max thought.

23
GALA
THURSDAY

The display of fireworks was simply brilliant. They shot up, blew up, and sizzled high above the island's heart – the great park. The evening sky was quite dark now. On the cool grass, people wove ribbons and did cartwheels with signs displaying the announcements of the night's festivities. This was the gala. Many different people made up the crowds that gathered on that night to celebrate, but all seemed to have one consistent hope. They metaphorically toasted to the island's prospects, and to the future. Lights flashed brightly and shimmered. Several strong men were tossing bricks of extending flame, toying with them with so little effort that they resembled cats playing with balls of yarn! The crowds that watched were amazed that the performers were not charred nor in the least bit harmed.

Kat and Rose had put the finishing touches on the dining area. People began to stream in to feast. Before the food was served, however, speeches were made.

"Thank you for coming to this wonderful event," started a speaker. "I introduce to you the night's premiere act of musicians, but first! I would like to say a few words."

Max was sitting near the park's border, closer to Rose's Flowers than to the stage where most of the action was taking place. Thus far, his Thursday hadn't been optimal. Quarry work was not easy work, and he was thinking of the adjustments he would have to make to last the summer. He sat sipping on some chilled drink, beginning to feel better, when he saw Paige and Colette across the way. He stood up, leaving his glass on the table.

24

THE WOODS

Relatives? thought Libby. *Some family.* She was now running as fast as her legs could take her through the foliage. She had very nearly just escaped with her life, with wild animals nipping at her heels.

An hour earlier, she had arrived at the address she had hoped her relatives would be at. She had bid farewell to the bus driver and walked to the door. The house was a nice country-style house that was done in an old Brisby style, and that meant elegance. However, no one was home. *Out for vacation,* read a note on the door. Then, an animal had growled, most likely a feral dog. Her spine was chilled. A tussle broke out somewhere nearby, and she started to run. The moon shone in the night sky above her, and her feet carried her, almost flying she ran, through the brush. Howling was heard. Finally, she felt safe and began to walk. Two hours later, she found the bus station. Nearby was a small hotel. She walked into it. The briefcase of Mr. Price sat on a seat inside of the bus, and the bus driver sat very still, looking at the fireworks going off on the other side of the island.

25

MAX AND PAIGE

At a time earlier, Colette and Paige had fully expected to no longer be on the island. Now, due to the briefcase crisis, they walked through the entrance gate that led them onto the gala grounds.

"How long are we going to be delayed, Colette?"

"I don't know. Father just said that an important issue had to be ironed out. It can't be too much longer."

Soon, the sisters sat down at some chairs near some drink stands. Max was not far away.

"Ned got you some flowers?" Colette asked Paige.

"Yes, but I don't think I would choose him."

Max didn't usually eavesdrop, but the girls' conversation behind him was obvious.

The Price girls. Chance seeing them here.

Max turned his gaze towards the stage where a band now played lively music. Colette too noticed the band, and she stood up. The musicians picked it up several notches, their renditions now celebratory.

"C'mon Paige!" Colette said.

Paige looked over at the band. Some instrumentalists had been so enthusiastically involved in the current music number that they had taken no mind to falling over and nearly injuring themselves, and others surrounding. Some members of the audience had risen up and collapsed dramatically.

Colette offered again. "Evelyn-Paige – to the hazardous stage."

Paige feigned disinterest, Colette sighed, and soon Paige found herself sitting alone. Colette rushed past Max and joined the enthusiastic crowd. Paige looked at Max. She adjusted the white ribbon that held her hair together artfully.

"Delivery of flowers," Paige said as she approached Max. "Your name?"

"Max," he said, moderately startled.

"Nice to meet you again, under different circumstances! Paige Price."

"A Price," Max reiterated.

"A Price," Paige said. "Family name is the reason I'm here. Don't get me wrong, Brisby is a fine place and all, but I know hardly anyone here, and it's so unfamiliar."

She then looked and saw people playing a sport on flat courts involving orbs.

"Bocce!" she exclaimed. "Have you ever played?"

"Never," admitted Max, and Paige caught his arm to lead him toward the courts.

26
BOCCE

Paige picked up an orb and tossed it from one hand to the other.

"What brings you to Brisby?" she inquired.

"Working."

Paige was not of the class that needed to work to survive, and Max intrigued her as a working-class citizen.

They stood together at a bocce court, illuminated vaguely by soft lights that shone amidst the summer dark. The concert was faint. They began a game.

"Where is it that you work?"

"At a quarry, contracted out by Green's Gem's," Max answered as he bowled an orb.

The two were becoming something – not colleagues, not strangers, but friends. A tree above them made a noise like *hush, hush*, and Paige dialed in an orb. Her focus was intense.

"I may have to drop into Green's Gem's to shop," Paige stated matter-of-factly. "Will you be there this week?"

"I will," Max said.

Soon the game ended. Paige won. They began another one, and as they did, Colette found them. She crossed over the neatly groomed lawn up to the small hill where Paige and Max now competed. The bocce courts were well maintained – flat, pebbly, and smooth. Colette's shoe dug into the ground and she spoke, making Max and Paige stop midgame.

"There you are. I thought that was you, the girl with the white bow in her hair."

"I'm Max," Paige's friend told Colette. "Care to join us?"

"Count me out," Colette said. "That show has made me weary. I did meet a friendly singer though. Might meet up with him tomorrow."

The bocce game continued. Orbs flew through the air, landing with various sounds. *Thud. Clink.* The music in the background had turned symphonic. Out of the darkness of the park there emerged a swooning conga line. Max, Paige, and Colette all turned and looked. Max dropped an orb. The line was coming closer and closer to him, and the group that made it moved almost in sync with the instrumentation that filled the night air. Colette recognized the person who led the line.

"Ned?"

He was wearing a disproportionately large crown on his head.

"Yes?"

Ned left his place in line to talk with Colette. Max stood very still. There were others who left the line also, Brisby folk who seemed to revere Ned for some reason. The rest of the people in the conga line continued their faltering path, moving by increasingly irregular intervals. Their enthusiastic voices faded into the background as Ned took off the crown and stowed it away.

"Want to play bocce?" Colette asked.

"No, not my thing really," came the reply. Then, Ned spotted Max. Colette's eyes drifted from Ned to Max.

"Wait," Ned started again. "I accept. Max and Colette versus Paige and I." He shined the crown with his shirt. Ned's cohort left his side to sit as spectators, eagerly anticipating what was about to occur.

The game began. At first, it seemed as though every competitor had equal skill. Despite Max being a newcomer to the sport, he and Colette won after a brief time.

"I demand a rematch," said Ned, and he got it.

Much was revealed during the second game. Paige let out a cheer for Max at one point, and Ned gave her a glare. He was a skilled bocce player, and this skill shone after he had faltered in the first game.

"I was just warming up," he said nonchalantly.

Max and Colette tried to replicate their success, but Ned was too good. He bowled an orb which in turn resulted in victory, and he stood next to Colette like a beaming hunter.

"I have a proposition for you," said Max then. "Best two out of three."

"Agreed," came Ned's reply.

Things became serious then. Max's confidence was solid, but Ned's was too. After a short time, the game seemed to be in Ned and Paige's favor, and so it came as a shock when Max pulled out from nowhere a winning bowl. The crowd went wild. Ned was not happy.

"Ned, you've been toppled," Colette sang.

"Positively beat," Paige added.

"Okay, girls. Laugh at me, but I say luck is all it was."

"Not really making jest of you, Ned," said Colette. "It's just a game, piccolo."

"Don't call me a piccolo. I say Max is."

"What does that even mean?" Paige groaned.

"Piccolo! Piccolo!" Colette tossed an orb from one hand to the other, having the grandest time.

Ned was over it.

"Where's my crew? I normally don't roll with you or your type 'o cat, Colette."

"Why aren't you more civil?"

"Civil?"

"Yes. Civil, piccolo."

"Because you keep calling me that!"

Max and Paige burst out with laughter. The Brisby folk gathered around Ned, and he unveiled the crown once again.

"The night is young," he proclaimed.

"Challenge me to a bocce match, Ned," said a crony.

"No! I'm done with bocce. Let's look for something else more worthy of our time."

"Let's," his friends agreed.

Before leaving, Ned stepped towards Max and said, "Buckroot has nothing 'gainst my type."

"The night is young," said a Brisbane.

Ned was wearing the crown as he joined his crew and disappeared into the night. The gala seemed to be over as soon as it had begun, and people began to file out of the park.

"It was nice meeting you, Max," said Colette.

"You too," said Max.

"Good times, although I might sock Ned one day if he keeps acting as he did."

"A sight that would be!" commented Paige.

Right then, a Rolls-Royce pulled up to a curb not far away from the bocce courts.

"There's our ride," Paige said.

After saying goodnight to Max, the girls got in the car. Max stood by himself as people walked all around him. He checked his watch.

27
AMBITION

Ned strode across the avenues of the park with his crew, seeking fun. They came to a little bridge. On the little bridge was a bench, and on the bench sat a figure. Ned's crown shone as the moonlight hit it, and the figure took notice.

"That your cap from Aldous?" It was Lawrence the captain.

Ned spun to look where the voice had come from.

"Captain," he said. "The cap would never do on a night like tonight."

"Is that right," said the captain laconically.

"Yes," was Ned's reply, but he was thinking more.

Captain, one day I will be clad in this crown professionally. When I take my rightful spot at the helm of Anne, I will be king of the fleet.

The captain said no more.

28
PAIGE AND MR. GREEN FRIDAY

When the city's clocktower had read eight in the morning, Paige Price arrived at the gem store. She had taken a car from the hotel initially, but now drove up to the storefront on a bicycle she had rented to explore downtown. She looked the part of a Price, with white gloves, ironed clothes, and pale red shoes.

She entered the shop through the glass doors and was greeted by no one.

She heard a sound and looked over to see a worker cleaning a window. Then, there was some rustling near the back of the store, and who but Mr. Green appeared.

"Hello," started Paige. "You must be Mr. Green."

"Timothy Green, yes. That's my name."

"I'm looking for someone who goes by the name of Max. A new hire."

"He was just here," replied Mr. Green. "Let me go fetch him."

Max was outside assembling some various tools for the days' work when Mr. Green had pulled him aside. Paige saw him very shortly after that.

"Here he is," said Mr. Green.

"Good morning," said Max politely.

Mr. Green left Paige and Max then, walking over to the repair counter. Taking a seat, he examined some carefully chiseled gemstones that had been spread out on the counter below Kat's necklace. The necklace had been placed on a little stand, and it seemed suspended in midair. Paige brushed her hair.

"Just dropped in to say hello. Our return trip has been delayed."

"It's good to see you."

"Why are you looking over there?"

"Say, is Ned around anyplace?"

"Don't worry, he didn't come with."

"That's a relief."

Mr. Green was concentrating on his work, and Max interrupted him when he brought Paige over to see the progress on the necklace.

"Here," Max was telling Paige. "This may be of interest to you. This piece of jewelry was once carried through trenches deep."

Max and Paige looked at the ornate piece. The gems shone.

"Have you heard the story?"

"No, of course."

Max smiled.

"This necklace was my great-grandmother's. My great-grandfather kept it with him while he was fighting in the first world war. An heirloom, and a piece of history."

"It's beautiful," said Paige, and she meant it.

"You see this brand?" said Mr. Green. He lifted the necklace to show the two where a symbol had been pressed onto it.

"It stands for Nigel's. The company has been out of business for decades." Mr. Green seemed distant when he said the words, and Paige and Max stood by, waiting for him to say something.

"Excuse me," he finally said. "What was your name?"

"Paige Price," Paige answered respectfully.

"A Price?" He offered a friendly handshake. "You are most welcome."

Paige beamed.

"Are you here to see the newest mining technology? Usually when a Price comes to visit, it is related to riches."

Mr. Green laughed out loud.

"Where would I go?"

"The quarry of course," came the reply. "Max?"

Max looked at Paige.

"To the quarry?"

"I will need to find my way back to the Hotel Empress by nightfall."

"It's not too far outside of the city," Mr. Green assured her.

"What do you say?" asked Max.

"To the quarry," Paige affirmed.

29

BRIEFCASE RECOVERED

A bus was returning to the transit center. Libby exited the vehicle, stepping down onto the sidewalk and disappearing into a crowd. Her only thought was to seek refuge.

Last to exit was the bus driver, carrying a briefcase. She took the briefcase to the lost and found, setting it down quietly on a counter.

"Mr. Aldous Price," sounded a voice into a phone. "We have something for you."

Shortly thereafter, Aldous had arrived. He took out of his pocket the briefcase key. Upon opening with no hesitation, he quickly scanned its contents. All seemed to be there.

"The case is closed and recovered," he said proudly.

Taking out a few documents in particular, transit papers, Aldous breathed a sigh of relief. The transit papers were necessary for his travel operation.

"Thank you much," said Aldous to the person at the counter.

Now we can finally travel!

Exiting the transit center, he looked off into the distance. He didn't know why he did it, but he sensed something ominous. Storm clouds gathered over the Pacific.

30
JOY

Paige spent the whole day at the quarry. Marco showed her around the grounds, and even gave her a tool to mine a bit. Max worked diligently. Soon enough, the day was drawing to a close, and some of the crew members talked Max and Paige into saddling up mules to ride to the top of a bluff.

"To watch the sunset," one assured them.

Max and Paige left their tools on a pile at the bottom of the rocky bluff, and in no time they were viewing the most spectacular sunset.

"A sight for sore eyes," someone said.

There was a viewpoint with a sign that read "Candy Mountain National Observatory," and Paige was thoroughly impressed. When it got dark, the group headed back into the city. They ended the evening at a dining establishment, ordering drinks and fruit. Joyous laughter could be heard from outside the place, and stories were told.

After the commotion had settled down, Paige parted ways. As Max bid her goodnight, his coworkers also left, and he was left to face the night alone. He promptly hailed a cab, and soon he was on his way back to the inn.

31

NIGHT

There was a car parked near Dazing Inn. The vehicle's color was black like the night surrounding it. Inside of the car sat three people wearing burglar masks.

"When's he going to get here," said one of them impatiently.

"Any minute, all right?"

"What's with these flowers sitting here?"

"Nothing. Pay attention!"

"Pay attention? Pay attention? How about you first pay your employee some decent sums!"

"I'll get the money to you, okay?"

"Quiet! I think that's him."

Out of the blackness emerged a solitary figure, strolling up the sidewalk that passed by the inn. It was Max. Suddenly the three got out of the car, ambushing Max in one fell swoop. He was tackled, and they all seemed to pile into a nearby rhododendron bush that gave way and broke underneath the weight. Leaves flew everywhere.

Soon enough, the anonymous figures lifted Max up, tied his hands, and threw him into the back of the trunk. The car left shortly thereafter. Kat went to see what the commotion was about. She saw the car leaving, looking out of a lit inn window, but soon went about her business.

Ten minutes later, the car pulled up to an abandoned warehouse. Above the giant metal doors that led into the place, there was a dilapidated sign that read "Jim's Smithing". Soon, Max was rushed through the doors and into a space that was lit solely by fire.

"Remember what I told you," said one of the masked people.

The other two shut the metal doors.

"No one's here, right?" came a whisper.

"No one would want to be here," another affirmed.

Max couldn't move. Not only were his hands tied, but two of his captors held his arms in lock place. They brought him close to a fiery stove, where old tools used to be forged like hammers and swords. Then, a metallic ringing sound echoed through the place, and Max shuddered. One of the burglars had brought out a hot steel poker and now brandished it.

"I am fueled by furious resolve," the burglar said calmly.

The burglar tossed the poker from one hand to the other, approaching Max. He tried to decipher what was happening, but he was unable to do so. What was going to happen? He could not fathom to guess, but it was not looking good. The poker was near his face now, and the heat emanating from it singed his eyebrow.

"Now, wait just a second!" The voice was one of the burglar's that held the captive in place, and as soon as the sentence was spoken, Max felt the grip on his left arm cease.

"I'm out. The agreement was to take the prisoner captive for questioning, not for whatever it is you're doing," continued the voice in a vindictive tone.

Then, its owner left, leaving Max and the two others standing there awkwardly.

"Hey!" started the one holding the poker. "This is fair and qualified justice teaching! There is a lesson that needs to be taught!"

Max had found a window of opportunity, and he commandeered the poker with his free hand and put the burglars on instant defense. A skirmish broke out then, and Max eventually found himself on the high ground to where he was able to rip off the masks of one of the burglars. The other had been defeated utterly, and he retreated to whence he had come. Max was actually trained in jiu-jitsu, and it showed itself on that warm June night. The mask came off, and Max let out a sigh of indignation. It was Ned. Ned thrust a kick, hitting Max squarely in the jaw. Ned ran for the poker, and Max decided to call it a night.

"I'll be going now," he said comically.

"Come back here!" Ned cried as Max escaped.

"That has to be one of the best fighters I've ever seen," said the other burglar.

Ned looked over and growled. "Let's go."

As he and his crony got into the car, the flowers were brought up again.

Ned looked at the speckled hibiscus that sat in the cupholder.

"I got them from Rose, the flower lady," he said with annoyance.

"You like flowers?"

"Rose was the one who told me where to find Max! She made me buy flowers for the information. She sold me these sparkling biscuits."

"What will you do with them now?"

"Give them to Paige," was the reply. "If Max doesn't get to her first."

32
KAT AND PAIGE
SATURDAY

Saturday morning arrived with an ominous foreboding. The storm clouds that had been brewing over the sea thickened. Though it was serene on the island, it was only a matter of time before its residents would be confronted with inclement weather.

At Green's Gems, Mr. Green was putting the last touches on the necklace for Kat. She stood nearby, watching as he meticulously cemented delicate stones. Max, looking rather worse for wear, stood by Kat. Despite the previous night's happenings, he reported for work like a professional.

"Almost done!" Mr. Green declared proudly. "Should have it finished today if there isn't a flood of customers, that is!"

Paige rolled up on her bicycle. Upon parking it outside of the shop, she walked in.

"Paige!" Max said.

Kat looked over.

"Max's friend," Paige said to Kat.

"Oh! How very nice," Kat said. "Did you two make plans for today?"

"We may have to," Paige said softly. "The storm delays our cruise ship and so I must stay until the waters are safe. The whole crew has their hands tied!"

"You could always go to the beach," Kat suggested. She was always one to seek alternatives to routine.

"Max will be working today," Mr. Green protested rather uncharacteristically.

"I'm not one to give references to Marco only to have them squashed."

"But Mr. Green!" said Kat. "Don't you think Max should be able to spend time with friends he may not see for much longer?"

Mr. Green didn't budge. "He has to be at the quarry today, I'm afraid."

"Quarry, beach. Forest, desert...what does it really matter, Tim? I think Max is going to have to respectfully decline the day's responsibility."

Mr. Green stopped his work, looked at Kat, and then looked at Max.

"Max...you can take the day off. Don't though, let Marco find out! We'll come up with something to say if he does."

"Youth!" Kat proclaimed. Whether she had referred to Max and Paige or to the concept in general, it was hard to tell.

Paige beamed, and soon she found herself sitting with Max overlooking the ocean.

At the shop, Kat leaned in and planted an appreciative kiss on Timothy's temple.

"Thanks," she said, looking over her shoulder and smiling as she left the store.

Mr. Green thought he was in love.

33

CAUTION

"Where's Ned?" Max asked.

"Ned? How should I know," Paige laughed.

"He is my nemesis, you are aware," Max said seriously.

"As far as I know, he is halfway across the island with his friends.

The tide rolled in peacefully. There was a faint breeze.

"What time is it?"

Max looked down at his watch. "Eleven 'o clock. Why?"

"I told Colette I would be at the Hotel Empress at four-thirty for her rehearsal."

"I see. Colette, Colette."

34

NED AND COLETTE

"Colette," Ned said. He was sitting in the back of a cab with her. The cab driver basically ignored them.

"Yes?"

"Is there anything else you'd like to see? We've toured the monuments, the museums, the parks…"

"I think that's enough tourist things for a time," said Colette. "Thank you."

"I know the best locales. Where did you say your sister was?"

"I can honestly say I don't know. Sometimes she goes down to the socials."

At that moment, they were driving by the gem store. Colette saw Paige's bicycle parked outside, with the telling white bow tied around its handlebars.

"I recognize it," Colette said aloud. "That's the bicycle she's been using to get around downtown!"

"You do have an eye for detail," commented Ned.

"Driver," said Colette. "Mind dropping us off at the gem store?"

"Indeed," said the driver, "I have to go around the block again!"

During the time it took for the cab to pull around to the front of the gem store, Ned went on a small tirade.

"Pshh. The gem store. You won't ever see me go into one of those places to buy anything. The whole operation is built on unfair business practices. Exploitative is what it is. Exploitative."

35

WHITE RIBBON

"It's lovely here," said Paige.

"I agree," Max said.

"I don't want to leave."

The storm clouds were gathering close by.

"We must," said Max. "It's four."

Reluctantly, they made their way back to the gem store. Paige's bicycle sat there waiting for her.

"She's not here," said Mr. Green inside of the shop. Colette and Ned stood talking with him.

"Well, hopefully she comes back soon. I'm off to the Hotel Empress to rehearse with Gerard."

"Gerard?" asked Ned.

"I met him at the gala," Colette said condescendingly.

Max faced Paige.

"I guess this is goodbye for a while," he said.

Then, as fate would have it, Max saw a movement inside of the shop and glanced through the glass window to see Ned. He fled.

"Where are you going?" said Paige.

"Paige?" said Colette upon hearing her cry, and soon she whisked her sister up and into the store where Ned and Mr. Green were chatting about the gem business.

Max ran through an alley and found a door that opened up to a staircase. He made his way up the staircase and found himself on a landing overlooking the entire gem store. Below him stood Ned, and Max ducked below the guardrail.

"We spotted your bicycle, or I did. It's hard to miss it with all that white ribbon on it."

"It needed flair!" Paige responded.

"Synchronicity that we should find you here," said Ned. "Synchronicity also that you were with Max earlier and now he is nowhere to be seen."

Paige stood silent for a moment, then spoke. "How did you…?"

Mr. Green was busy repairing the necklace, but sensed that Paige was looking at him. He looked up just in time to see the angry look she shot him. He cleared his throat.

"In any event," Ned continued, "We have an appointment at hand."

"I'll call a cab," said Paige. Before she left the shop, her eye caught the gems that now shone bright in the necklace. Mr. Green had finished it.

"That necklace," Paige commented, "it's so gorgeous."

"Yes," said Colette. "I've already bought you a birthday present, if that's what you're hinting."

A birthday present – Ned had overlooked one.

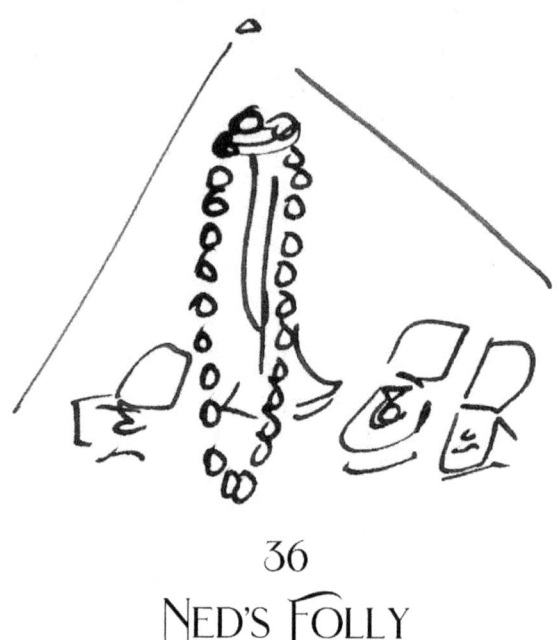

36

NED'S FOLLY

Paige walked over to the alley, looking for Max. She sighed, hailed a cab, and motioned for Colette and Ned to board. Ned stole the necklace as Mr. Green spoke with customers. Max saw it happen from his bird's eye view, and his mind raced. Ned had pocketed the heirloom swiftly, and Paige stripped the bicycle of its ribbon and tied her hair up into a bun. Max started down the staircase to confront Ned, but it was too late.

Beep-beep. The cab rolled off the curb into the lanes of traffic, and Max was left standing in the literal and figurative dust. Paige, Colette, and Ned sat in an uncomfortable quiet as the cab driver looked at the GPS that gave directions to the Hotel Empress.

Max waved down a taxi, and got in immediately.

"Where to, boy?"

"The Hotel Empress," said Max coldly.

"The Hotel Empress," repeated the driver.

The city flew by Max as he watched out of his window. The storm clouds continued to build. The cab came to a screeching halt ten minutes later, and Max got out, putting his feet squarely on the ground below him. The atmosphere around the famous hotel was grand. Torches to repel insects had been arranged in an aesthetic manner around the grounds, and ancient sphinx statues seemed to stare at Max as he made his way to the entrance. He would get that necklace back.

37

CONFRONTATION

Max entered the hotel. It seemed he was being drawn into the place like a marionette. On Tuesday, Max had gone into the hotel with roses. Now, he carried only with him derision. He quickly found the room where Colette was rehearsing.

BRISTOL'S BROWN EYES HAD BEEN FULL
OF SURPRISE
ON THAT MORNING IN TRUE BLUE
SEPTEMBER
THEN, SHE HAD BEEN TROUBLED AS HER
MIND WANDERED COUPLED
WITH THOUGHTS
WITH THOUGHTS
WITH THOUGHTS

"Laying distant her memory!" yelled Max. Ned turned, the necklace clinking in his pocket.

"Max! Max!"

Max chased after Ned. Colette and her new friend Gerard as well as Evelyn-Paige stood bewildered.

"What is happening?" Colette demanded.

"He stole a necklace of great value," Max was saying, "and it needs to be returned."

Ned was stubborn as Jules the mule.

"Prove it," he said. Paige looked at him.

Max stopped.

"Let's go get some fresh air, Gerard," Colette said evenly.

As they left the room, a ballroom in fact, Ned protested.

"I wouldn't steal," he said.

Paige stood still.

Max tore after Ned. Like a fired blank at the start of an Olympic triathlon, the competition kicked off.

"What are you doing!" shouted Paige. It was too late. Ned had run up a stairwell, down a hallway, and into his luxury suite. The door slammed in Max's face.

Trifles.

38
ROOM SERVICE

Ned was sitting quietly on his bed, looking at the necklace with a hint of malice, when a light knock disrupted him.

"Room service," came a voice.

Ned strolled up to the door, looked through the viewer, and saw a hotel employee holding a tray of lobsters. Max waited with bated breath in the hall, hiding himself from Ned's view around a corner. Ned took a lobster in one hand,

and before he knew it, he was face to face with Max. The employee shrieked, the door was slammed, and Ned walked backward before tumbling onto his bed. The lobster hit the floor.

"Allright Ned," Max said. "Hand it over!"

Ned responded by opening up the doors that led to the balcony. The wind outside blew the curtains wildly. Lightning cracked in the sky. Paige, at a loss, had joined Colette and Gerard.

"I love you, Gerard," Colette said out of the blue. Paige heard something. She looked over. Ned had jumped from the balcony onto a nearby spindly tree. He climbed down the tree, and Max followed him, mustering strength. Amidst their folly, Ned knocked over a torch. Colette and Gerard went back into the hotel, citing the lightning for their decision. Paige tried

to get them to notice the feud happening nearby, but they were caught up in the throes of a new romance. Fire now spread through the foliage surrounding the Empress, but its instigator saw it not. Ned had already darted away from the hotel and now was jogging at a steady pace towards the natural park. Max followed, and so did Paige. Her white clothing made her look like a ghost, and soon enough her and Max had cornered Ned in an alley. Removing one of her slippers, Paige threw it at Ned's hand to knock the necklace free. It worked.

39

A RAVEN

Paige recovered the necklace in a sweeping movement, and right after received a smack across the face. Ned lowered his hand, and Max held his derision tight. The necklace fell out of Paige's hand onto the cobbled walk below, and a raven picked it up immediately after.

"They like shiny things," a peddler commented. Paige, Max, and Ned all stopped.

Max looked to the sky. Lightning crackled as the raven flew away with a measured flap.

"That necklace was incredibly...shiny."

The fire glowed in the distance. The hotel manager called the fire department.

"I need it back!" Max said to the peddler.

"I will say," the peddler continued without missing a beat, "the ravens around here will always nest around the natural park. The food left by tourists is too much to resist."

Max had heard everything he needed to. He thanked the peddler and headed directly to the park. Ned followed and so did Paige, and the peddler went back to minding his own business.

The raven landed on the tiger statuette at the gate of the natural park. The fire department drove by as the stars shone above. Sirens wailed as thunder rolled. Max arrived at the gate of the park and rushed through it. He didn't see the raven perched atop the snarling statuette. Soon enough the raven had left its spot, flying free above the park.

"What are the chances?" Max said under his breath.

Flap. Flap.

Max looked to the sky. The raven was attacked by another of its kind, and the necklace fell from its talons into a nearby pit. The fire department rolled out hoses as the fire spread into the park. Paige's shadow was illuminated by firelight, and she chased after Ned to escape. Ned saw Max climbing over a small border, and Ned pursued.

40

BURNING BRIGHT

Thump. Thump.

The two fools fell into the pit simultaneously. It was not too dangerous of a fall, but Max did twist his ankle. Green eyes moved glowing around the dark. Paige stood at the edge of the border, looking down. The trees above her burned. Flames illuminated the chasm. Black stripes were lit by orange light. Tigers.

Max felt a hot breath above him. Incapacitated with a crippled limb, he looked up and into the eyes of a fully grown and very bothered tiger. Gemstones shone nearby.

"First to the prize," came a voice.

"Ned," said Max. "It's not worth it."

A tiger cub ran by. Its mother roared.

"I can get it!" Ned proclaimed.

He swooped in and grasped the necklace, but the mother tiger was incensed. She went after Ned, and Ned dropped the necklace out of pure terror. Max recovered it, and the fire department came not a minute too soon, lowering down hoses for Max to grab onto; he had Paige to thank for that. She'd assisted heroically with the efforts to extinguish the flames and had directed the fire crew to her friend down below.

Ned was next to be rescued, but this proved more difficult. Getting him separated from the vengeful grip of the mother tiger was no easy task, but Max proved his integrity by assisting the crew in their efforts.

41

A GEMSTONE ARMY

"Heave! Heave!"

The army of firefighters shone like gemstones that night. The flames were soon extinguished, Max was swept away to the care center for treatment, and Ned slipped off into the darkness. Paige remained at the natural park, caring for animals affected by the fire. Then, the sky broke. Rain poured down in sheets, and not a few firefighters saw the painful irony. Charred piles of blackened memory were soon all that remained of the fire. Paige stood in the rain. Two firefighters called her to leave in their truck. She hopped in. Glancing down at her palm, she shook her head. The necklace sat there, untarnished. It had fallen out of Max's pocket as he had been carried onto an ambulance.

"Where to?"

"The Empress," said Paige.

42

CONSEQUENCE

The rain was falling in large droplets when the firefighters dropped Paige off at the hotel. Mr. Price was there to greet her, giving her a hug that almost brought her to tears.

"What's happened to your face?" he asked.

Paige brought her hand up to her cheek. She had almost forgotten Ned's strike.

"It was Ned," she said plainly.

Aldous dialed a number.

43

RECOVERY
SUNDAY

Morning light cascaded into the upstairs bedroom where Max now lay recovering. He was back at the inn. The medics had treated his slight burns and cast his ankle. Now, he lay horizontally on a bed, head propped up on a pillow. Outside, the storm clouds had diminished completely, and the window that had been opened let in a fresh scent.

Paige stood quietly at the inn's door. The automatic bell let Kat know that someone was there, and soon they were talking in the parlor. Paige's father stood outside, dressed professionally in a suit. Jay sat behind the wheel of a parked Rolls-Royce, and Colette and Gerard were laughing in the back seat.

"I have to make it quick," said Paige. "Where's Max?"

Max saw someone wearing heels, a pencil skirt, a white blouse, and a cocktail hat. Then, he saw her face smile.

"Paige!"

"My heart is warm to see you safe," she said. "I have to leave, though."

She took the necklace from her pocket and set it on a table near the bedside.

"I can't believe it," said Max.

In the harbor, the captain stood at the ready.

"The sea calls," said Paige. She kissed Max on the cheek, leaving a pink imprint.

"See you again sometime?"

"Most definitely."

44

AFTERMATH
MONDAY

"Mr. Green," said Kat the next morning. "I don't know when Max will be at a hundred percent."

"It's okay," Timothy said. "I will let Marco know. Say, did Max give you the necklace I repaired?"

"Oh yes, and I need to thank you. It looks marvelous."

"Oh, good! I almost thought that someone had stolen it."

"Max the scoundrel," said Libby.

Max looked up. He was sitting at a table on the Dazing Inn's lawns and had not expected to see the green-eyed girl there.

"Mistakes are made," said Max.

"That's not good enough," Libby replied.

"Max the scoundrel?"

"Unless you can prove otherwise."

"I know just the way," said Max. He smiled.

45

CONSTANCE

Three months later, Max found himself boarding a cruise liner that would take him home. A small crowd had gathered near the shore, and among them was Kat, waving goodbye.

"Tell your mother she is missed! Say hi to Penny!"

Constance was the name of the liner Max left Brisby on, and everything about her bespoke the Price name, save any actual Prices. As for Max, he prospered after that summer on the island. He had mined treasure for Libby, Penny, and Paige, and gathered enough for himself too.

He watched the island fade into the distance. The ocean sparkled around him as dolphins jumped out of the water. "Onward," he said.

46

RETRIBUTION

Ned wore a uniform.

"What are you in for?"

"Arson," Ned said. "Plus, crossing the most powerful man to frequent Brisby."

"Who's that man?"

"Aldous Price."

The outlaws stood in a line, chained together to a dozen others who worked to restore the natural park to its former glory. Plants blossomed. Rose was there as well, working to make things better. The outlaws sang.

THE SAILORS' HOPES WERE CRUSHED
ALL CRUSHED
OUT ON THE OPEN SEAS
HIS BOOTS WERE FILLED WITH TALES
WHERE HE'D WALKED
YET NEVER COULD HE BE FREE

HIS WOMAN WAS LIKE SORROW
DANCING
OUT THERE ON THE ROCKS
FOR ALL THE CAPTAINS TOOK TO
GLANCING
AT HER BRIGHT GOLD LOCKS

HEAVE HO! ALL YOU SAILORS
HEAVE NOW!
THE LIGHTS FAR OUT YONDER GIVE WAY

Dan Kubishta

Let's climb once again our severed
ropes
For most our fine maidens have left,
left us laden
With naught save one hope for
some hope

Officer Lt. Tin supervised the group. He looked out from a vantage point high above the ground. Polishing the buttons on his uniform, he watched a cruise liner leave the island.

47

THE END

The final glimpses of Constance were being done by the people who had stayed silent on the harbor. They saw the minuscule white speck cross over the north horizon line, disappearing into the distance. Then, they left, walking up the boardwalks, onto the beach, towards the city. The day's light no longer was illuminating the parks and filled avenues of Brisby. The skyline twinkled as night drew near, like a glistening star. If one turned to look out at the sea, standing at the shore, a beautiful sight could be seen. It was a sunset, shining bright.

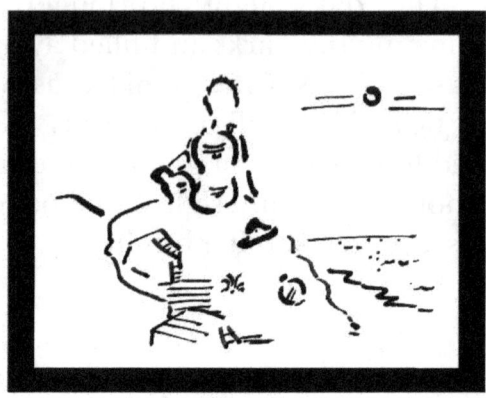

EPILOGUE

Kat placed the necklace on a stand next to the parlor. An oil painting hung above it, depicting a soldier sitting on a beach. Music played softly.

DAN KUBISHTA

www.ingramcontent.com/pod-product-compliance
Lightning Source LLC
Chambersburg PA
CBHW060228180626
46813CB00007B/2996